The Champ And Other Short Stories

By Jonathan Colón

Table of Contents

(*Enter*)

Charles' Three Day Weekend

Prologue

This story is about a man who lived in cloudy weather, but felt the warmth of the sun behind it. Charles kept a journal; what proceeds contains excerpts from this journal.

It was the Thursday before the three day weekend where Charles worked. He soon got home. There, he sat down to rest from the day's work. He proceeded to read the newspaper with coffee he had bought on the way home. Although Charles many times felt pained with mild torment; he, proceeded forward and never let it get the best of him. It was late summertime and the city where Charles lived in was bursting with activity. Charles didn't have any children; therefore, he would adventurously look for things that would bring delight to his life alone. Amidst difficulty Charles never lamented, this is not to say such things were not heavy upon him. With almost bravado he would continue forward.

Charles wrote:

Dear journal,

You very well know that I am a hard worker who doesn't complain. I have written this before. Things in spite of their glimmer seem bleak. Although, an extra day's rest wouldn't hurt.

It was now night and Charles fell asleep with a promising good feeling. It was about his three day weekend to come. It was now Friday morning. Charles had woken up peculiarly refreshed that morning.

Charles was later to write:

I felt like I could take on the world. The beauty of my surroundings could only be surpassed by the feeling that I was in a good place. I walked by, and even a fellow my age with what seemed to be his grandson gave me a slight wave. The temperature of the city seemed to perfectly compliment the notions I was having. A clear bustle of activity was somehow evident as I walked through the streets. I must say, there was even a visiting sense of love and wonder.

Charles had proceeded with his day. Charles could not hide a smile as he walked towards the coffee lounge.

Charles had written about his short time at the coffee lounge:

I sat there drinking on a dark cappuccino. I was at ease. Everything seemed melodious and the cappuccino was not so bad either. Whip cream on top are you kidding me? As I exited out the coffee place I was greeted by a crisp wind that had been traveling amongst the day's warmth. It was a little revitalizing. It certainly made me fasten my pace to the local park where I had planned to sit down and bask in the serenity.

At the park Charles had the chance to reflect. In his time of reflection, he encountered the seismic thought which was: this lovely life beautified by the proceedings of those whom live it, has been being lived this whole time.

Charles had written about this:

These things were undeniable. As my heart kept beating so did the beauty; warm, and bursting of all things. I had come to discover a deep down feeling that we all cared for each other at least in a minimal form. Somehow, this was as evident as a cheering crowd for their sports team.

Charles continued with his day. It was now getting dark. The Friday night was vibrant with possibilities and bountiful opportunities. Charles had gone to a bar. The gentlemen next to him were in a rather festive mood. One of them had exclaimed to his friend, "The night is young!" He turned around to ask Charles, "Don't you agree?" Charles responding, "Yes indeed." Charles was slightly intoxicated. When he made his way outside the bar he had looked up to the dark sky and saw a small and very fast meteor shower. He soon made it to his car.

Throughout his drive home he sang along to the music he had listened to as a youth. Charles sang away.

That night he wrote in his journal:

All throughout this day I walked with glee: with a determination to live; to enjoy things. It was the equivalent to a first kiss leaving one feeling the promising of more. It was almost a laughing matter. Yes, a cause for celebration.

After finishing writing in his journal he quickly felt both exhausted and triumphant. Lo and behold; the feeling of an even better day awaiting was there present, as Charles soon went to sleep.

It was now Saturday morning. Charles arose from his slumber wanting to take on the day. He felt the teasing feeling of romance. He felt like taking on the day; and being successful at doing so. The occurrences of the day remained as they slowly lingered away. Yet, for that moment it was substantially felt. Charles had given a rose to a woman from work. She accepted his courtship.

Charles wrote about her:

She is an educated, professional woman, held in high regard not just for her looks. It was in the afternoon we met together; where, I gave her the rose. If I didn't know better I'd say she was blushingly smiling.

Epilogue

Charles continued to conquer the days to come. It was something he always wanted to have. It was why he continued to breathe, to be able to live, and not frown at everybody. It was something he always wanted to have: a three day weekend.

The Champ

(Urban Literature)

Prologue

There are some, whom in the midst of adversity crumble. Yet, there are those that even in the midst of utter chaos triumph. This story is of a man named "Heavy". He is one of those people that never quit. Before a habitat that only knows one rule: survival of the fittest; he triumphed. Heavy was a man very worthy of respect.

Chapter One

Henry was later to be called "Heavy", his street name. He acquired his street name at the age of fifteen. One day in his first year of high school he had rode the school bus home, just like any other day. He was thinking of homework the whole way back to his neighborhood in the ghetto. The school bus had stopped at his stop. Many times he would think of how much pain it was to live in poverty, but he did not despise growing up in his neighborhood. Quite the contrary, he loved his neighborhood, the people in it, the sights, the sounds, those times when he was made smile. He liked smoking marijuana with his friends. They had been friends for a long time. It was this particular day; after school, that his friends asked him if he wanted to join one of the major gangs of the city. He had replied, "You know I'm down". He was to get jumped in which consisted of several gang members punching and kicking the "newbie" for about thirty seconds.

It was in the evening after school that they all met up at the park. Henry was ready to fight back which was allowed. All three of his friends were there to jump him in along with two older gangsters whom were there to observe. The initiation had begun. Henry's friends had all gone through the same process. He knew it would be him next. He swung back. He fought courageously; as if a heavyweight in a title fight. Thus, after the thirty seconds were through he was given the street name "Heavy". In spite of being thrown to the ground in the fierce barrage of punches being kicked as he was on the floor, the thirty seconds were finally over and he was greeted approvingly by the older members, the gang itself, and his friends. He was now one of them: a 49th Street Hustler. Him and his friends celebrated -later on that night- at his friend's house with liquor. There was laughter, clinking of beer bottles and the talk of girls. It was if they were all finally on the same level. Drunk, he had walked back home now a 49th Street Hustler.

Chapter Two

The 49th Street Hustlers were notorious for being the baddest most paid gangsters throughout the city Heavy lived in. Throughout all the 49th's history: they beat down, murdered, and robbed any person deemed weak to their eyes. It was the way of the ghetto it was the way of the 49th to show no mercy. To them, they saw anybody outside the gang as prey. Yet those within the gang were held in high esteem. Drugs, their usage, and their being sold were iconic to the Hustlers. So was murder. It was around forty years ago that the 49th Street Hustlers was formed. It was an agreement between three gangsters whom were friends that marked the beginning of the gang. One was a murderer, one was a drug addict, and the other was a man all about making money. They all agreed to utilize each others' strengths for their benefit. This occurred on the corner of 49th Street and Gibson; at night, in the very city Heavy and his friends lived in. Throughout the years the Hustlers grew in numbers and became a force to be reckoned with.

The people selling drugs at the time started to see the 49th Street Hustlers as a threat; this being, because of their rising numbers and their business pursuits. Not only did they receive money from robberies; they were robbing stores, pimping, and -on top of it all- selling drugs: everybody in the gang received a bit from each dollar made. The money also went into lavish, raucous parties; where there would be drugs to all those that wanted some; and, every member - including the women- receiving the gun of their choice. These guns; and the souls they took, solidified the presence of the 49th Street gang within the city. The peoples outside the 49th became groups. These groups joined together: forming a challenge to the 49th Street Hustlers. The lines were drawn. As the defenders started to fight back many people died. War broke out. Many friends and family members wept at the loss of the person they knew. Many sought revenge accomplishing it. From then on, the battle was perpetuated. This battle was present, and kept alive even in times Heavy was living in.

Chapter Three

Heavy got home, radiant for he was now a Hustler. He knew that on Monday he was going to be the talk of the school. He had made up his mind to ask a very pretty girl he liked to be his girlfriend. He soon went to sleep. The next morning he had woken up and greeted his mother. His mother said, "Why hello there youngster you came in late last night, is everything good?" He replied, "Yes momma" and began to eat what she had made him. Heavy's mother said, "You eat up now, I want you to grow up to be big and strong and be real smart like a scientist". He laughed. "Finish all your homework too" she said. "Okay momma" he said through a smile.

Heavy and his mother had gone through a lot, but they went through it together. Heavy's father had passed away when he was little. In the worst of times they found each other. In the worst of times the understanding people of the neighborhood were there too. The best of times happened there.

Chapter Four

It was now Monday and Heavy was waiting for the school bus. On the bus, he met up with his friends. On the way there Heavy had mentioned to his friends about his plans to ask the girl out and they were happy and proud for him. At school others had other plans for him. During lunch, one of Heavy's schoolmates defiantly approached him. His schoolmate said, "I heard you's a bitch ass Hustler now" Heavy replied, "What the fuck did you say?" the schoolmate said, "Fuck you". They began to fight. With the high school students gathering around, they saw Heavy unleash a torrent of punches to the face of the schoolmate knocking him down. Hovering over him Heavy told him, "What the fuck now muthafucka!" It was as he said this that the friends of the schoolmate came around swinging at Heavy. Heavy's friends quickly joined in. It was a four on four fight. Girls started screaming. Heavy and his friends relentlessly fought away only to be broken up by the high school security. Heavy threw a swing at one of the campus security breaking his nose, blood pouring out. Heavy was later to be expelled. Heavy had to let his mother know that he was expelled explaining everything that happened. She told him something that made them both smile and even laugh a little, "Son, they can't punish you for having a good right hook." What proceeded was the two enjoying a nice time talking the time away together. They laughed and smiled. Heavy's mother even told him more about his father.

It was starting to get dark outside. That's when they heard the doorbell ring. Heavy went to see who it was. It was the girl that Heavy wanted to ask out. She said, "I heard what happened at school. I think you're bad. Your homies told me that you're a 49th Street Hustler now." Heavy told her, "Yeah I just got jumped in the other day, Friday night." She said, "They also told me you wanted to ask me out." Heavy replied, "Yeah it's true. So you want to be my girl?" She replied, "Yes."

Chapter Five

Heavy's girlfriend had a street name also: Sugar. Together, the world seemed to lightly glow. It was as if there was a soft audible hue to things. Although Sugar was Heavy's girlfriend, he couldn't resist passing some young pimpin' at her. He asked, "Let's just say if we were older and I had a car, could I be your pimp?" She said, "Yeah, of course" then quickly asked, "Could I be your ho?" Heavy responded, "Yeah." Full of mischief Sugar asked, "And all the money would go to you?" Heavy said, "Yeah, and a little bit of it to the 46th Street Hustlers and Hustlettes." They continued spending the day with each other; kissing, talking, and at times being silent together.

It was now dark outside as Heavy kissed Sugar goodbye and headed back home. Approaching his home, it reminded him that he was expelled from school. It was how his day was spent that brought a smile to his face along with the feeling that things were going to be alright for him. A 49th Street Hustler, dreams of money rushed through his mind; reassuring him, that he was going to be alright. He planned on speaking with the older gangsters about making money; as many his age had done so before.

Chapter Six

The young Heavy had already been introduced to his girlfriend's dad. Although Heavy didn't know it, Sugar's grandfather was one of the original three that had formed the gang. Along with the other two of his friends, Sugar's grandfather was still alive. It was customary for a younger Hustler to approach any older gangster when wanting to be presented with the chance to make money. In spite of his age, Heavy was ready and willing to pick a gun and rob someone. If someone outside the gang was deemed a problem; worthy of death, then he would get killed: ninety percent of the time, it was at the hands of someone that got paid to do so. The other ten percent was because the habitat was so.

At Sugar's house Heavy walked inside and sat on the couch. Sugar had told her dad that Heavy wanted to talk to him about something. Sugar said, "Go ahead, tell him" Heavy proceeded to say, "Sir I wanted to talk to you about making money, I want to make money." Sugar's father said, "Oh, okay the youngster wants to make some cash. So you want to get down with the get down, hot dang. Well you is alright young man. You scared of the police locking you up?" Heavy replied, "No." Sugar's dad asked him, "What would you do if the cops were close by about to lock you up?" Heavy replied, "I'd kill them." Sugar's father said, "Cool. You like drugs?" Heavy said, "Yeah." Sugar's father said, "Hold on I'm going to get us some weed, we goin' smoke and I'll tell you all about it."

The three smoked weed as Sugar's father explained to Heavy the different types of ways to get paid; what to do, and what not to do for each. Sugar's father said, "Again youngster, the drug slangin' and robbin' aint the only way to make money. I know about what happened at your school, you being expelled and all that. I aint no hypocrite, anybody up in this ghetto would love to see you make it through high school, and do okay with that money. Remember that." Heavy said, "Yes sir." Sugar's father shook Heavy's hand and said, "That's right. Just stay in school, but yeah you can get with cash flow. You goin' need a gun, I'll let you know when you get to pick one." Sugar's father left. Shortly after, Heavy made his way back to his house.

Chapter Seven

The time came when Sugar had let Heavy know that her dad was ready to talk to him about the gun. Heavy and Sugar walked back to her father's house. At Sugar's house, her father greeted Heavy. He said, "Wussup youngster, today is your day." Heavy said, "Oh yeah." Sugar's father let out a small chuckle. He said, "Well us three goin' go for a ride to the spot; get the gun you want." Heavy replied, "Cool." They arrived to one of the houses where someone could obtain a gun. Sugar's dad had explained that the young man needed a gun. Heavy had picked a semi-automatic pistol. He put it inside his pants and let his shirt hang over it. Sugar's dad said, "Aw hell yeah." They left the house and drove back home. Heavy was now "strapped".

For two weeks, Heavy wasn't going to school. He spent all his time selling drugs. He later enrolled in another school. During those two weeks he had made a lot of money for the 49th Street Hustlers; he made a lot of money, for himself. He was buying things he wanted to buy; he was eating more; as well as getting drunk and high with his friends. He had caught up quickly in his new school and was able to pass his classes. He was sixteen now and enjoying summer vacation. Heavy continued to sell drugs, carry a gun, and hang out with his friends. He was still with Sugar even though they were going to different schools.

The summer went by quickly, filled with; activity, mischief, and celebration. It was during these moments no suffering existed, things were good, the love that at times seemed was not there was alive and present, and the support that was there for each other was prevalent throughout all the ghetto. Whom else better than one's brother, one's sister, one's neighbor to feel those feelings that made one feel that it wasn't so bad. Whom else better, than with the people these feelings were caused by; the very people, these feelings where felt with. Cigarettes were smoked. Shots were fired into the air. The summer had come to an end as those before.

Chapter Eight

Heavy felt better. A Hustler, Heavy was living up to the 49th's notoriety for making money. In his sophomore year at his new school, he was to encounter another young gangster by the name of Lace. Lace was from the gang that rivaled Heavy's. Lace was a pimp. It was how he got his money. One of his prostitutes knew that Heavy was from the 49th Street Hustlers. She knew this because she knew about Sugar. Lace soon found out about Heavy and where he was from. Instead of rushing to fight him, Lace set to plot Heavy's death.

Lace somehow found out that Heavy was raking in money from the people Lace sold drugs to. Heavy had achieved this by lowering his prices for the same drugs. When Lace found out about this, it sent him into a fury; his plot to kill him was arrived to quicker then he thought. Lace had planned to drive up to Heavy's city bus stop and shoot him as Heavy came out the bus. Alas, Heavy already knew about this. As he exited out the bus, Heavy was pulling out his gun. As the bus drove off; Heavy was searching everywhere for Lace and his car; information gathered upon a warning about him.

Heavy quickly spotted him and ran up to Lace's car. Lace received a bullet to his shoulder, the second bullet piercing his head. Heavy quickly threw his gun into a street sewer, ran through an alley, and upon turning the corner walked home. The ghetto Heavy's neighborhood was found in had felt another execution by the hands of a 49th Street Hustler. Sugar didn't have to ask Heavy about it. They spent a short while together and soon kissed each other good night. Heavy soon went to sleep glowing of self love. Sugar's dad was later to offer Heavy an opportunity to deliver bulk amounts of drugs to different houses. Heavy accepted.

Chapter Nine

Heavy soon found himself graduating: one of the most paid gangsters his age; eighteen. His mother was utterly proud seeing her son graduate. As the amount of drugs dealt with increased, so did Heavy's pay. Heavy found himself in a world he had never experienced before. Heavy enjoyed his own apartment driving around the city in his car. Even with many women being attracted to him, his heart never left Sugar. The love they had for each other still bringing waves of warmth through them and all things aglow. Even with Heavy enjoying his adulthood, with different women; Sugar in all love forgave him. Yet, what was to become of the next year of his life would prove to be one of the toughest. Lace's little brother; had vowed to find the murderer of his older brother having the people, money, and guns to do so. Lace's death had sparked an uproar to the 49th Street Hustler's rival gang ending in a war. It was one of the bloodiest wars in the 49th and their rival's history. It was led and started by Lace's little brother.

Heavy valiantly struggled and killed through it all: surviving. After eight straight months of this war, it finally died down the 49th Street Hustlers victorious. Heavy proceeded to take over a large part of the city's drug clientele including an immense portion of the rival gang's clientele. It was as if the city itself was supporting his every breath. Lace's little brother had died in the midst of the war. In spite of all the challenges he had faced he never gave up, he never quit, and was victorious double fold; for not only had he survived, he had earned his respect.

Epilogue

Heavy and Sugar's enduring love blossomed into them getting married. Heavy became a youth basketball coach. Fulfilling the words of Sugar's dad, the ghetto was proud.

Nirvana Achieved

(Science Fiction)

Prologue

This story is about a group of friends. They all had a way to reach a nirvana without having to pass away.

A group of four friends whom hung out together: two of them a couple; the others, were composed of two guys and girl all had their qualities, they all had their strengths. Day knew that night would come around of course. Yet, even in darkness they knew how to resort to a nirvana. It was something worth taking a second look at. It was when the couple were together; the highest feelings of nirvana would be felt. They all knew what each others' means to nirvana were. They even had conversed about how it feels. They all had similar experiences and thought processes. They were friends so much they shared their feelings on Nirvana.

One night they were all hanging out at one of their apartments. One was listening to music, the other was smoking marijuana. One of them was sitting there graffiting his blank page notebook. The couple were sitting there hugging each other. They saw time gently flow by in each other's embrace. Where would they all go? It was like a state of mind; or, a state of being which brought forth intensely good feelings and thoughts.

Each of them had found out what they were doing, the couple being together, the graffiti artist writing graffiti, he whom smoked marijuana, and her listening to music: was the portal to each of their nirvanas. Their nirvanas all had a similarity which was feeling as if each one of them were taken to another planet; a planet, similar to ours. Our's and their's alike, they had similar contemporary contexts. One of the only differences between our planet and theirs was time: their planet being within the future. The coinciding planet was achieved more times than not. A gift from the future was almost always given. It happened to occur, that all of them pitched in their findings. They became bearers of the source of the fact; that, the future was bright.

Epilogue

They continued to hang out and resort to their nirvanas. They continue to bring great gifts from the future.

Farewells in Smiles

(Romance/Noir)

Prologue

Raymond and Kimberly were a couple whom had said goodbye to each other, ending their relationship: in all triumph.

Do you know, the multitudes, of composition that lies beneath the caress; the simple symbol that one is not alone? The receiver finds himself the giver, for she found herself before the same reminder. It is undeniable and inevitable; very, unavoidable the brisk frigid notion that one is alone. It is of a warming glow to find oneself in the embrace; of the one whom you love, that very person whom loves you also. Those moments together; reminders that amidst the frigid we must combat; there are times when one's love is of aid to such battles. Lo and behold, because the brisk lingers abroadst; the two, finding refuge in cherished moments, birthing blissful forget. For in those moments, the seemingly prevailing cold was championed over. Not a trace of the daunting loneliness could be fathomed; thus, it did not exist.

Why must one deny, the plethora that is present before those bound in love; delights in large quantities received from one's love. The wonder, the adventure, the pleasures, and times good: received. Many harvests to be enjoyed by the couple, their labor consisting of the things centric to that couple. Together, they enjoyed the spoils of their victories, basking in the soft warm hue; resulting from their expressions of love. These delights; these pleasures; rising and becoming of a concentrated decadence. Certainly, bliss would arrive to carry the two off into a state where the only thing present was the love between them, and the cool refreshing serenity. It was the very warmth of her body, the sweetness of her embrace. The reassuring strength of his, was coupled with his love for her. Her love was everpresent; they proceeded to love, to give, to engulf each other in what was their's and their's only. Even when they were away, the vibrant remembrances of moments shared together would arise within them.

Chapter One

Raymond was 29 years old. He worked at a local health clinic. He was a RN there. Raymond was steps away from becoming a workaholic. He had immersed himself in his work; in the weekly schedule. His sense of medicine was slowly becoming an obsession. At home; it was as if, he never left the clinic. Raymond was very altruistic. He took pride in his work. The way Raymond had saw working at the clinic was that he was supporting a larger cause which was: all things medical. Raymond would admit –in all honesty- it was a small contribution; but, no one would be able to convince him otherwise in regards to the fulfilling sense of purpose he received showing up to the pharmacy everyday. At one point, one of the doctors there asked him, "You really take this job seriously huh?" Raymond had responded, "Yes." Before the doctor had returned to his office; he told Raymond, "Keep up the good work."

Torrents of immense magnitude behind that simple embrace they found each other in. Both receiving, always keeping their love alit, kindling it with such simple acts as the kiss. Simple acts but yet enormous in meaning. A broad mass was what was being conveyed to one's love; her, the very one whom loved him. The dawn's airy warmth shining upon the two for they had withstood the threats of having to proceed alone. As innate as the very breath, the man and his woman were found together: united. The love between them; expressed, the very kindle of the fire: they kept; this fire, reaching intensities; that fire ablaze. How could residing amidst being alone victor over what is two-fold; those two individuals united, conquering anything that might be harmful. It is as innate as the breath, to venture forth to find her; her that would become one's love; in all similarity, her accepting the courtship. Such occurrences found amongst times and times, found throughout and beyond all horizons.

Chapter Two

Kimberly was 28 years old. She was the newly hired RN at the clinic Raymond worked at. After the brief meeting where Kimberly was introduced to the staff the head doctor mentioned, "let us all make her feel very welcomed" and the meeting had ended. This was around the time work and research into things medical had grown to a full-fledged obsession for Raymond. It became the focal point in Raymond's life. It started to show up in the workplace; this obsession. Kimberly had noticed different exuberances on Raymond's behalf; but, saw it as intriguing rather than a cause for alarm. Kimberly would by the most part keep to herself at the clinic. She was very sharp and very professional. During lunch breaks she would be social, but when it was time to go to work Kimberly would proceed to concentrate on the work at hand.

Raymond proceeded to assess himself. He had discovered he had a hollow within him. A limited self esteem was only part of his strife. His sense of fulfillment slowly began to corrode. He was presented with a startling concept: What if what I'm doing is not enough? He knew he was of the medical field; helping others heal and feel better. In spite of this, he felt as if something was not right still. Raymond continued to feel lacking and hollow. It had dawned upon him that he was stricken with loneliness.

Kimberly and Raymond talked more often. Raymond was impressed by her clearly noticeable altruism. Their talks were mainly polite short addressing of each other; nothing more. Short as their chats would be; Raymond was able to see that Kimberly was altruistic like how he was. As the time went on Raymond had become sure that Kimberly had a "bad girl" side. This made him begin to see her as interesting. This was most likely due to the fact that Raymond had an edge himself. Somehow, the short polite talks they had; diverted the attention elsewhere, away from his strife.

(Raymond)

Yes, I find myself in quite an inner predicament. I have never felt so empty. It is like 80% of me is mere air. You want to know something? That Kimberly, she's so interesting. A rose with thorns, yet the structure of a true altruist. I must admit, during our chats; our brief addressing each other with small talk: I was elsewhere. I found myself drifting into an escape from my menacing current mind state.

(Kimberly)

Hmm, what to say about Raymond. I can tell he's smart. Yes he did in one occasion get a little hyperactive. He was mentioning something in regards to the cause which is the medical. The sincerity in his words diverted the attention from his ushered physique and directed it to a man who cared.

It is the very song; enchanting, that arose between them. Just as the rising tides; just as, the rising warmths what they had together was acknowledged by both. It is only the very time; an era of what was the two and the two for each other that arrived as the very shining of the sun. This wonder evoking song played gently amongst them, for they were good to each other and their times spent were reveled in. Nothing horrific was about, nothing pain. The song of the rising intensities between those two had ushered the melodies of the motions; that would unify them in love. Their love began to surface; shimmerings, towards the day they could give to each other the very symbols of their love for each other.

Chapter Three

Somewhere along the line Raymond had found something that stood out amongst many things. What Raymond encountered was that: those conversations he had with Kimberley were not upon the terrain of torment. Quite the contrary, these were conversations; times together, that were not disagreeable to either one of them. On many occasions they were quick to remark on what was just said. They were very smart; and soon, their conversations began to extend. The two drove a very nice intellectual conversation. At times it was invigorating. Of course this occurred on the clock and they had to cut each other short on numerous occasions. They both found each other encountering very light and gentle notions of longing for each other's company.

Raymond had proceeded to acquire Kimberley's phone number; they soon had, many conversations. Upon hanging up, more and moreso they felt the longing for each other become stronger. They enjoyed those conversations, they enjoyed their moments together. It was made known for both; that, both their pains resulted from loneliness. Kimberley had several bad relationships so had Raymond. Never had they extended anything vile to each other. Their conversations were delightful surprises to each other; each instance supporting what they had in common. Their times together became too short for what they could've been.

(Part of a phone conversation Raymond and Kimberley had)

Raymond – Hello Kimberley?

Kimberley- Yes this is her.

Raymond – Hi this is Raymond. How are you?

Kimberley – Good. How about yourself?

Raymond – Oh I'm good. Thanks. You could have noticed me a little off; a little to on at one point. I wish to address this and apologize.

Kimberley – Let me apologize for being a little short.

Raymond – Apologies accepted

Kimberley – Yes same here

Raymond – Tell me if I'm wrong; but, do you like rock?

Kimberley – I love rock.

Raymond – Me too. You know screaming is a good therapy?

Kimberley – Oh stop

Raymond – Scream some vocals at the top of your lungs

Kimberley – Then need some cough medicine?

Raymond – You got me there

Kimberley – Need some cough medicine?

Raymond – Yes

The two continued their conversation. They were presented with notions of how good it was to speak with each other; and, feelings of how good it felt to spend time with each other. Decadent was the thought that they were so good for each other. The day had arrived when they found the augmenting attraction between them well present. They found each other by a stream within a meadow. They were in love with each other. On that day, they became a couple.

Chapter Four

They were in love with each other. Everything seemed gently bright. They were amongst their glow. Their love didn't cease to amount. They felt as if each sign of love given to each other burstingly supported and augmented their love, their relationship. They took pleasure in showing love to each other in numerous ways. Their love was constantly given constantly received. They mischievously ventured forward. Everything was aglow.

Raymond had escaped trekking through what was loneliness and self denial. Kimberley had acknowledged Raymond and his worth. She was the shining answer to his loneliness. As for Kimberley, her denial of a "good guy" existing was made obsolete. Kimberley's loneliness was vanquished by Raymond. Together, they championed over all ail; all the while, giving to each other.

They shared and felt the wonder the promising next moment: together as children mischievously about. The promise of the next moment and what it would bring. Certainly it could not be of detriment. For he and his love proceeded through a kind world; much different from the frigidities of times alone. It was such times that led them to develop a longing for each other when they were away from each other. She found herself in his strength; he basked in her reassured calm. Their love and all the times they had felt those decadent and rich feelings that blossomed from the so fertile grounds of their unity, symbolic gifts to each other. They found theirselves before these; dancingly ablaze, lighting the next adventurous step, the beckoning next moment. Their adding to the kindle, the malacies abound were certainly not fathomed for they loved each other and longed for each other when they were away. They longed for the exquisite moment: together.

Chapter Five

They proceeded to enjoy the harvests of their benign labors, and sowing the seeds of the showing; the giving to each other. The bounties arising from the fertile ground which was their proceeding together, their love for each other unfleetingly present. The evanescing warmth between them upon the night's arrival. The waves of these reaching the shores of the rising memories of: the feelings felt; and, the gifts given beneath the sun's guiding their very about. Those memories bringing them through the night; those, kindle for what they shared.

(Raymond)

I am so in love with her. We have never faced anything malignant this whole time. I had rid myself of the descent I had embarked upon. We are two lovers, medicinal and interesting to each other. We agree with each other. We do not ward each other away. What we have could not be any purer and beautiful.

(Kimberley)

I love him. He is pleasantly fitting to me I to him. Nothing ill has arisen between us. We frolic through time: together. What we share; as well as what we express to each other is free of any tarnish or blemish.

Chapter Six

All throughout their relationship the reoccurring thought that arose within them was of marriage. All roads were leading to it. In a culminating point in their relationship; they found theirselves one weekend afternoon in the most perfect of times and settings: beside the stream in the meadow they once visited. It was the perfect setting for his proposal of marriage and her acceptance. Instead, they had agreed to not see each other anymore. Raymond had said, "I guess this is where I ask you to marry me but I have no doubt that we both feel the same. To go any further on our relationship would ruin things." Kimberley responded, "Yes I know what you mean. To go any further would just tarnish things" Raymond said, "You read my mind. They enjoyed their last laugh together. Victoriously, with smiles on their faces they intentionally ended their relationship.

Epilogue

Raymond and Kimberley never entered into marriage. The two of them were comfortable with not going into marriage. It was not foolhardily on their behalf; nor, was it a gamble. They did so, because the two wanted to give to another: the opportunity to experience love.

June 24th

Prologue

This story is about a day out of the ordinary in it's quality. A quality felt widespread. What follows are individuals' accounts and experiences of this day.

Chapter One

Hello my name is Leonard. I am forty-five. I must, absolutely must tell you about June 24th. It was a sweet day. It seems as though the sun was burning extra hot that day. I felt like a little kid that day; like a child in a candy store. It even seemed like I had a greater ability with the women. That morning I could even hear it on the news announcer's voice that the day was going to be very nice. I literally stormed outside with much elegance. A very attractive woman walked by. I almost scared myself at the realization that I could take on the world in one day.

Leonard had written in his journal the next day:

"I was jumping out of my skin. I can say that I truly felt a surge of life crash through me. I had an espresso that morning. Sitting there opportunity frolicked through my mind. I had never felt so opportunistic and mighty. I had never seen opportunity so vincible."

In all confidence Leonard went for a drive. He had heard on the radio, "for the people to exhibit caution in not being over festive" and "remember to take a lot of pictures on such a day." On the freeway Leonard, let out a, "pooha-pooha!" So much was his glee that he tapped the steering wheel.

Leonard had written in his journal:

"Everything was going so great I knew that any second my heart was going to burst. I was almost singing at the top of my lungs."

Anymore and Leonard would have started speeding down the highway at a pace even quicker than what he was already going. He happened to have passed by the city's sports stadium. At one of the stoplights a man approached him and said if he wanted tickets to the baseball game at the stadium. Leonard told him yes; paid the scalper the unbeatable price the scalper had asked for and proceeded to the game. A man stormed the field and slid on his belly just over home plate. The referee motioned "safe" and had exclaimed, "Safe!" Another man hadpoured beer on his head. The crowd was on their feet in a standing ovation to the pitcher of the home team's last pitch. The home team ended up winning seven to one. The city was in a benign uproar. It was as if they were in a tactful collective madness in celebrating. The motions and the proceedings were only enhanced by it being the 24th of June.

Leonard wrote in his journal:

OUR TEAM WON JUNE 24TH!

Why hello, my name is Leila and I had a really nice time on the 24th. It reminds me, of the twenty four in "twenty-four seven."

Leila had written in her diary:

"I am truly not the superstitious type, nor do I believe in the tooth fairy. Yet, that day was very pleasant. I had a nice time observing my plants I had on my porch. If I didn't know better I'd say the plants were basking in my care for them."

Sitting there on my porch close to my plants, I felt serene. I was awed at the day and it's ginger progression. The day had increased in warmth. Hours had gone by and it was now noon. It dawned on me that I had spent hours in reverie.

(Anonymous)

I had gone out on my first date with this girl that I really like. We had lunch together. More than once I looked up to find her pleasantly looking at me; a smile on her face, a couple of times. I knew she was having a great time as much as I was. Lo and behold, we both wanted to continue dating each other. The approaching evening only promising the chance to see each other again and have love flourish between us. It was something we both wanted; something we both wanted: with each other.

A couple proceeded to walk through the park holding hands. They felt an urgency to express love to each other. As they walked; together, they were truly appreciating every second of it relishing every moment.

That day, their love intensified. They proceeded to be clothed in happiness, the happiness they made each other feel.

The sun had set and it was now evening. Even though the sun had set it did not impede the wonder; the beauty; and the plethora of opportunity: that the night brought forth.

(Julius)

Aw man, June 24th at night? Are you kidding me? It was so happening. It was so burstingly alive. Oh I partied like if it was the 24th; get it? Me and my friends went club hopping. The music; the vibe; the whole nine yards it was all so instigating: a positive instigation. I heard women happily screaming over the music, I tried a flaming shot, and I danced with a group of girls. It was pandemonium. At one point I seriously thought there was going to be a riot in the street. Julius is my name and I'm 26. Oh I partied hard. I know I wasn't the only one. My friend almost fell off his barstool. I very strongly feel; that it was two steps away from outrageous. I had to go different ways from my friends and what they were doing because one of the girls I danced with gave me a very sexy wink. My friends had clapped and waved goodbye from across the club; as I, walked out with her.

Hi my name is Missy and I'm 28. It was about six or seven o' clock p.m. as I felt a warm refreshing feeling and went outside to walk around. Even though it was night, it was very warm. I could hear birds chirping through the trees. I began to truly cherish my walk. I felt a love for everything and felt really sassy. I didn't doubt; I didn't challenge the way I was feeling. The night and it's mystique had lured me to the coffee shop a couple of blocks away from my house. As I sat down with a flavored coffee extra whip cream, I dove into a heavy intrigue.

(Poetry)

The night

It's kindness,

It's provoking

Exciting notions of the libertine

Providing glimpses of what could be

The fulfilling of these,

In all their decadence

The only reason I had walked back home was to get my car and greet the nightlife. I had never felt so victorious as I did driving back home.

Epilogue

The 24th of June was to stay on the minds and within the hearts of all those that had enjoyed it's bounties; citywide, for a long time to come.

Burdens Of Mine

(Noir)

Prologue

This is the story of a man and has encounter with hardship: he never gave in to it.

Chapter One

Greetings, my name is Edward I am forty-six. I have resided in my neighborhood for quite some time. My job; which I stayed loyal to was in a warehouse. I even had dinner with the boss and his wife. I have a few friends from the warehouse. I found that working with friends made the time go by quicker.

(Edwards Poetry)

That time clock

Presented with all these glances

Even more, the end of the shift near

That time clock

Supporting my labor

An avenue to payday

The very amount which kept me breathing

How am I not to hold

At the very least some form of endearment

That time clock

Proving my labor

Proof that I worked

for the company I work for

That time clock

There everyday just like me

The warehouse; would it lead me to the riches and luxuries? This would occur to me every once in a while. More than on just one occasion these thoughts would be drowned by me regaining focus on the work in front of me: soon finding myself addressing the work at hand. I know I would be showing up to work the next day. Many years of my labor were engrained on that time clock; even if it could only count hours. Soon, it would be another year of this.

Chapter Two

Bright morning, I had come to find. Not so hot just bright; if that makes sense. I would frequently read the newspaper and have a cup of coffee.

(Edward Poetry)

Coffee in the morning

It's not too hard to figure out

That coffee pot

Sending me off to the rest of my day

If coffee pots could talk right

In those cups of coffee

There would be the promise

Of another day

Another day to be part of

No sugar

Those cups of coffee

Like all the rest

Started my day

And sent me off to enjoy

A night job worker's day

No creamer

But I'd say yes to a newspaper

The morning ritual

Starring coffee pot and the rest of the day

How could one

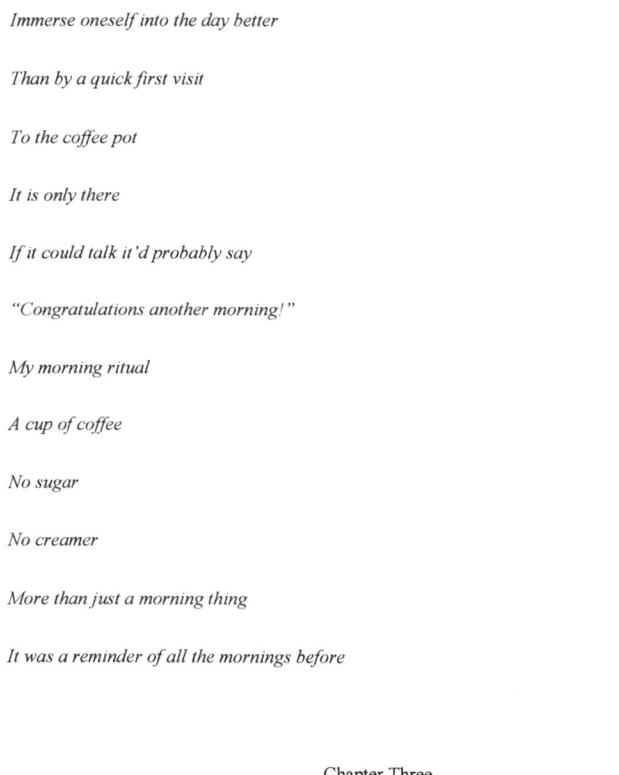

Immerse oneself into the day better

Than by a quick first visit

To the coffee pot

It is only there

If it could talk it'd probably say

"Congratulations another morning!"

My morning ritual

A cup of coffee

No sugar

No creamer

More than just a morning thing

It was a reminder of all the mornings before

Chapter Three

I guess you could call me one of those fortunate ones that couldn't complain. I found myself submerged in this feeling; when presented with, the beginning of my descent of sorts.

A Lost Friend

1.

It was something more than an unpleasant surprise. I got home from work waiting to be greeted by my pal. What I am talking about is my dog I had had for more than a decade. Man's best friend. He kept me company when I found myself alone. He would always greet me every day as soon as I opened the door.

2.

What I had walked into; when I entered my apartment, was his dead body. It was just sitting there motionless. You would have expected me to rush to come up with a way to dispose of him. He was a medium sized retriever. Instead of it's disposal I was just simply aghast. I wasn't expecting such a sight until years later. Jet was his name. Just a puppy; even then, he was very responsive to me. He would sleep alongside my bed.

3.

I soon found myself pained. He just looked so serene there; and now, no Jet. It's not like I didn't have human friends, but that I kinda of saw him like a friend. The usual way such a scenario would be is: someone opening the door, turning on the light and seeing cockroaches scatter; or, a surprise birthday party from friends and family. This was of a man's pet, it's corpse: no more man's best friend.

4.

Granted, it wasn't the death of a loved one or friend; I just wasn't expecting it. A painful thought went through my mind: What am I going to do with his doggie biscuits? Should a man lament so much over a dead pet of his? I thought. I quickly went to dispose of him. Another thought arose in my mind when disposing of it: should I cremate him, say a eulogy? Once in the dumpster, I went up to my apartment. I sat there calmly and picked up a magazine.

Chapter Four

At the warehouse, my friends were at their usual midshift shenanigans. Normally I would join in, or say something supporting their low key raucousness. This was not so for me. Honestly, I wouldn't give one more thought to Jet's death, but I did. It soon became what I was thinking about the most. It was such a nice dog. It proved to be more than just garbage as I had told myself to see it. This lament I was feeling was strong for me. I was to find out my lament was soon to be coupled by devastation.

No More Dinner Guest

1.

I took it as a great honor to be invited to have dinner with the boss and his wife. Years of dedication, good work, and very little tardiness had brought me the recognition that led to dinner at the boss's place. I remember the talk of the boss's good looking and young wife lasting a great part of a break amongst us workers. I had made sure I didn't gawk at the dinner. We all had a good conversation and there was even a toast in my honor; recognizing my contribution to the company.

2.

We continued to converse until it became late. Making my way out the door the boss's wife gave me a very provocative look. I didn't respond as I was still in no gawking mode. The look spoke volumes. It was a look that screamed unhappiness with her older partner: my boss. This wasn't a surprise to me. Many stories were passed around on how she only married him for the money. My boss was the type of boss that would frequently step out his office and walk through all the employee stations; sometimes he would pass a short word of encouragement.

3.

A week after the dinner party the boss -on one of his walks- visiting his employees; was acting very odd. The boss did not do a routine visit once, not twice, but three times. The thing about it was that in each of his walks; he was literally glaring at me. He soon asked me to have a little talk with him in his office. He had told me he didn't tolerate intra-job relationships. He continued to talk about his wife cheating on him with me. This was a complete lie; and I had tried to argue my case. He continued with letting me go.

Chapter Five

I couldn't believe it, although it was an obvious lie I was used as a pawn to establish the grounds for my boss's divorce. It dawned on me that I was fired because the boss's wife was unhappy with him. I was fired a good employee with the toast of champagne supporting this fact. My job, looking forward to clocking in job; what fed me, I would leave feeling I did a great job around the last minutes of the shift. A good chunk of my day, going to sleep exhausted; an exhaustion not acquired from toiling in mindless things; it was an exhaustion acquired from doing warehouse labors: gone, all on the boss' inability to keep his wife.

Chapter Six

I always got along with my father. He didn't have to tell me he was proud of me it was evident. In my torment I saw things bleakly. What followed was a week of not coming out my apartment. I had isolated myself from the working world; the happily married world, the so on and so forth world. I had found a warm, almost tactful feeling seeing a picture of my father and me. In that picture, my father was beaming his pride for his son. I remember those moments with pops; walking along, me having a grown up conversation with him even in young age. A second skin he wore, it was of the pride in me; his, love for me. I saw him as a "big guy" even in adulthood. Those moments were hard to forget. That picture was very refreshing and reassuring.

Chapter Seven

It just so happened that I received a call from my father. It was not what I had thought it would be. The nature of the call was humiliating, ruthless, and very unsupportive. He had rubbed my failures and "lacking what it takes" in my face. As if making his words, words of veracity; I defiantly became the nobody nothing failure he had so vividly portrayed me as. I even told myself, "I'm a loser." I exclaimed, "I don't know what two plus two is! I really don't." I soon hung up with him.

Chapter Eight

Solace was what I resorted to. For a week I did not step outside; no morning ritual; I became estranged. Who else better to rely on then the one whom can see calamity for what it's worth. I decided to kill two birds with one stone. Waste money at the casino; and, have monumental fun there. To the casino I went. It was a casino in particular. This casino had very nice advertising I'd say. The advertising of this brand new casino consisted of pretty women, an array of cash being thrown everywhere, and a minor raucous in general: every time. I was lured in. The hyper, blaring of the slot machines only added to the excitement of the whole casino. My fever for money was along the lines of those superb commercials. I was so enthralled by it all: I quickly, almost instantaneously became a frequent gambler. Yes, I gambled almost the totality of my funds: Cheap thrill high price. At least, for those moments; I wasn't such a bad employee, such a bad person, such a good lover.

Chapter Nine

I knew, that I could rely on that never tardy to work gentleman. The friends from work I tried to contact had in the most evident of ways denied all my seeking their company. No more human friends; but myself, and the solace I provided myself. I remained that loyal warehouse laborer, my acknowledgement of something good in a world gone wrong. I casually worked my way to the cd player. I found myself listening to a song from my high school years: all the memories and glories behind it still intact.

(Edward's Poetry)
The good the
Blissful loss in the song
Part of those songs that seemed to
Linger
that seemed to be
Constantly playing in the background

The celebration of our youth

With the endeavors of ours

Solidified and backed by these songs

It only took me to

Times still in me

Listening to that song reminded me that I may not know what is going on, but I know the difference between calling myself stupid and calling my strife stupid.

Chapter Ten

In utter desolation I provided myself the means to withstand these woes. I was found in a supporting stupor at the lowest of my descent. Television seemed to comfort me. One night, flipping through channels; I came across a family drama drenched in the most audacious and fake scenarios. The comforting television brought another presentation; arrived to by flipping through the channels once again. It was a special on bees that make honey. I almost punished myself for watching it. My adventures in television viewing reached; pinnacle, preposterous heights. Knowing I would never watch one I sat there and watched a cooking show. I was consumed by a period of sheer disgust.

Chapter Eleven

I was almost hysterically laughing. I must confess, the burdens did not harm me. The sound of my laughter marked the end of my hardship. It was the end of a calamity ridden life; the start, of a life free of such woes. I had proven myself worthy of a life without them.

Epilogue

Never again was Edward to face such hardship. He continues to live a trouble free life.

The Trident Movement

(A Fictitious Research Paper)

Prologue

The following is a research paper written by a university professor; published in the scientific journal he writes for.

I must say it is not my usual disposition to address things such as drugs. Yet, I feel as though this particular drug deserves a second look. The drug I am speaking of is: Trident. Some would call it genius. Others, would quickly try to change the subject. This is a drug that comes accompanied with it's own movement. A movement inspired and driven by it's effects.

The first time I had heard of the drug was when two of my colleagues drifted into the subject after a very prolonged debate. I quickly chimed in my interest. I was recommended I do some research on the drug. I didn't know it at the time, but it was the start of a very informative and rewarding expedition of sorts.

I began with the World Wide Web. I was interested in both: books on it; and, any news that might have been printed on the subject. To my surprise, I was made aware that there was an entire movement based on the drug. Credible sources had all stated that the movement lasted two whole decades.

At the time, I wouldn't have been able to explain why I was so interested. At first glance, I deemed it sheer myth. As I sought deeper into the subject the mystique of it all began to fade and I began to discover cold hard facts. The chemistry facts all seemed very solid. I had noticed the figures and key topics in exact form within three different reputable sources. The resonating and driving question was: How could such a thing be kept so secret? I was later to find out that instead of a widely syndicated periodical; an article on it would appear in a monthly poetry journal in a college. So on and so forth for all the forms of communicating the news. Through my research pursuits and efforts I had accumulated a shocking amount of information. It is my intent to inform others about this drug and it's pertaining movement.

What follows is a brief summary of the effects elicited when taking the drug Trident. The user would begin feeling a cold, but not a frigid or piercing cold. Sensations of actively rising, yet suspended would occur. The mood would be in a state of light; not heavy, happiness. The general definition of the concept: "bright" as in lighting; would be continuously present as a sensation. Kind thoughts towards one's fellowman were common. Numerous accounts indicate that the aforementioned feelings were very intense. Yet, the intensity did not reach extreme, detrimental, or excessive levels. The high would usually last eight hours. It is appropriate to note that the more that was consumed the stronger the feelings; yet no potential for overdosing whatsoever.

I was very fortunate to unearth an episode of a public television show. The topic in this particular episode was about Trident. The episode was very crucial because it showed three persons on it; as well as, these individuals being interviewed. The individuals consisted of two men and a woman. The woman had got up and started to slowly; gracefully; and lightly move her arms as if dancing. One of the men spoke to the host/interviewer. He asked, "Perhaps you can do the interview early?" The host responded, "Yes by all means." What follows is a part from the interview written verbatim. The name of the guest was Caesar, and had been interviewed for fifteen minutes. Caesar had said, "I feel as though I am suspended and floating. I am entirely aware that there are many things, happening around me. I simply love the big environment I'm in. I want everybody to feel a simple light good feeling as I am feeling right now." It had also shown the second man very gently going into the audience and silently shaking people's hands; him, waving to others; and, putting his closed fist over his chest and nodding "yes" for a good three seconds.

I had also come across footage of: a governor on it during a speech; two different celebrities both on it; and the lead singer of a band on it during one of their concerts. It was recorded that during the 20 years of The Trident Movement an entire culture across the world about it had been formed. Only certain individuals came across Trident and the dialogue, events, actions, and works of and about it. Only a very small amount of chemists knew how to create it. To this day, Trident is still being made and used. I was privileged enough to be one of those whom have tried it.

Concludingly, things like Trident should be embraced and certainly not denied. To produce something beneficial to the world is a pursuit worth pursuing.

The following reference table contains a list of all the links, books, and sources that provided information crucial in the forming of this research paper.

Epilogue

The professor continues to teach. He continues to write for the scientific journal.

The Delicacy

Prologue

The following is the story of a married couple and their vacation to an exotic location.

Chapter One

James and Monica were a married couple. They had been married for a delightful thirteen years. They didn't have children. Thus, both of them were employed. Although they were happily married they did have their "ups and downs". Nevertheless, they stayed together, lovingly making it through and on to better times. James and Monica loved to travel. It was something they utterly enjoyed; it was something they enjoyed together. Almost overwhelmed with work; the two would cherish times alone, and also times away. Their honeymoon was the first time they had traveled. The first time they had traveled –outside of their honeymoon- was a weeklong escape. They had enjoyed it dearly. Between them, they had finished three bottles of champagne.

James had always wanted to visit The Islands of Bliss. It was a very popular place to vacation to and stay at one of their luxurious hotels. The Islands of Bliss were a group of five islands. The weather there was always hot in the day and humid throughout the night. At night the sands of The Islands of Bliss would stay warm; the sound of peacocks could be heard; and the aroma of various flowers would intoxicate the air. Yet, it was the sea life that the Islands of Bliss were known for most. Ten types of fish that were edible would pass through the waters of the islands. Many sport fishermen would go there just to fish; although, it was very common for them to enjoy the islands' other delights. A very large waterfall was located on one of the islands. The waterfall's water would first fall into a large pool and then make its way to the ocean. It was in this pool where a certain type of shrimp was found. It was the largest type of shrimp that existed; the size of a crab. These shrimp were completely white and thick. They were very docile. One could even touch them -when they would swim to the pool's shore- as they liked the attention.

All the chefs of the Islands of Bliss were skilled in the preparing of this particular type of shrimp. For a price one would be able to try the world renowned delicacy. When eaten; it would launch him or her into an intense and pleasurable four hour experience. The experience consisted of living within the ocean, yet still on dry ground. One would be able to see different marine life swimming by accompanied by feelings of soothing warm refreshment. It brought feelings of slowly swimming through water, as one walked. Intermittently, there would be feelings of glowing; waves of heavy heat would pass through the body. Sensations of weightlessness would arise and would leave one feeling as if being pulled by a strong current.

Chapter Two

It was now close to James and Monica's fourteenth anniversary. They were to take a vacation to the Islands of Bliss. James had mentioned it to Monica before. Monica was thrilled to hear about them vacationing to the islands. She had; quickly rushed into James' arms and gave him a hug. They were soon packed and ready to leave to the airport. After a ten hours of flight, they had finally made it to the Islands of Bliss. It was about six o'clock p.m. Island of Bliss time. The couple was greeted by a beautiful panorama and the islands' famous climate. They caught a taxi to their hotel. They soon checked in. They kissed before leaving to walk through the city. Monica was awed at the beauty of the city. Along the way, James had bought her a souvenir. They had proceeded to walk about. Once back to their hotel they spoke about the walk and soon went to sleep.

Chapter Three

They had awoken refreshed. They soon headed out to walk the shore of the island. Along the way; holding hands, they saw a beach side diner. They proceeded to order the famous white shrimp. Upon ordering it the waitress had turned around and made a gesture with her hand to the woman at the cash register. The woman at the cash registered had called out to the cooking crew and they began to applaud as it was custom when anyone had ordered the famous shrimp. Other people there at the diner looked around in bewilderment and curiosity. Soon, James and Monica had left the diner.

What follows is James' personal account of the experience.

(James)

It was about thirty five minutes when I started feeling the effects of the shrimp. Slowly, the things around me began looking softer. Then, before I knew it everything was warm and I felt as of liquid. Not only this I felt an immense pleasure within me. It was as if I was gracefully moving through water. The sun's rays piercing through the waves above had all the things in the city aglow. Two hours later the exquisite feeling within me doubled. Fish were all about me. A school of seahorses curiously approached me. I was in unison with the movement of the sea. There were no oceanic predators. The city, it's buildings, and all the people were still there. Towards the end of the experience, my wife was wearing a diamond and pearl studded crown. This was the most beautiful sight I had ever seen. Thereafter, the experience soon ended.

What follows is Monica's personal account of the experience.

(Monica)

Wow, I truly do not regret eating the shrimp. It was so heavy the feelings I was feeling. It was so beautiful. The fish swimming around didn't cause an alarm. I was truly moving as if floating through water. I felt moved by a slow; soft; and, gentle current. Breathing was not a problem. The city being there was calming. I felt soothed. I felt the warmth of the day's sun. At the end of the experience everything sea related drifted away. The peculiar thing about the experience was that towards the end I saw my husband with a crown of diamonds and sapphires.

Chapter Four

After their experience they headed back to their hotel room. It was there that they had talked further in depth about their experiences. James had told Monica that at the end of his experience he had saw her with a crown studded with pearls and diamonds. In utter surprise Monica had told him that she had seen him with a crown as well. It was a breath taking moment for both of them. They had agreed that it might mean something; and so, went back to the diner to ask about it. There at the diner they had explained to the woman at the cash register about it. With utmost seriousness, the woman at the cash register had told the owner of the diner. The owner of the diner had come out and began to explain to them. He had explained that such an occurrence did mean something. He had told them that although rare, sometimes the white shrimp experience may bring insight on things. He had asked if they were married and they both said they were. He had explained to them that them both seeing each other with a crown was testament of the strength of their marriage. They soon parted with the owner of the diner; walking on cloud nine. Back at their hotel room they renewed their vows. It was on their anniversary.

Epilogue

James and Monica made it back home, their marriage reinforced by their vacation to The Islands of Bliss.

Times of a Couple

(A Fictitious Memoir)

Prologue

What follows is a light hearted memoir from a woman. It is about her late husband.

They were the greatest moments of our lives are moments together.

Ever since college I was very attracted to Robert. He was a jock in high school I was a cheerleader in high school; always going for the home team. We had ended up at the same college. I always thought I would be able to really entice a good man.

Everything was love everything was light being with him. We were really walking on the clouds. He would shower me with gifts. We were one and it was nice that way. It was as if we shared feelings him and I.

Everyday felt like a walk in the park, a higher, warmer walk in the park.

We were together and in love.

Epilogue

She was later on to get married and enjoys an ongoing marriage.

Cars Passing By

(A Parting Poem)

As I drift off to slumber

I will not forget the days of this last summer

The cars passing by

Are the undulating waves, rhythmic

Reaching the shore

Lulling me to sleep

Once more

(Exit)